Christmas Cheer
Gayle Buck

Also by Gayle Buck

Tempting Sarah
The Waltzing Widow
The Holybrooke Curse
Season of Joy
Hearts Betrayed
Chistmas Cheer
Old Acquaintances
Mutual Consent
The Chester Charade
The Desperate Viscount
Lady Althea's Bargain
Fredericka's Folly
Love for Lucinda
Lord Darlington's Darling
The Demon Rake
Lord Rathbone's Flirt
Miss Dower's Paragon
Belle's Beau
Cassandra's Deception
Love's Masquerade
The Righteous Rakehell
A Magnificent Match
The Hidden Heart
Willowswood Match
A Chance Encounter

The Fleeing Heiress
Lady Cecily's Scheme
Cupid's Choice
Lord John's Lady
Honor Besieged

Chapter One

The first snow fell softly during the night. Lady Hallcroft woke with a feeling of well-being which was only heightened when she received a note on the tray with her morning chocolate from her lord, suggesting a morning ride together. Lady Hallcroft felt a surge of happiness. She sent back a reply in the affirmative. She finished breakfast and rushed through her toilette, anticipating the ride on horseback.

Lord Hallcroft awaited her downstairs in the wide entry hall. He was already attired in a riding coat and breeches. He leaned against the finial at the foot of the stairs, one elbow laid casually across the top of it. At the sound of her hurried footsteps above, he straightened and looked up.

When he caught sight of her running down the stairs, his mouth lifted in an appreciative smile. "There you are, my lady. I was afraid you would wish to remain abed on such a chilly morn."

"Not I," exclaimed Lady Hallcroft gaily. She looked down into his upturned, handsome face. Her heart turned over as it always did whenever she saw him. She was still pulling on her gloves and she was somewhat breathless from her dash as she joined him. "I wouldn't miss a morning ride with you for worlds."

"I'm flattered." Lord Hallcroft swept her form with a swift glance, taking note of the heavy woolen cloak, tied at the throat, which covered her velvet-trimmed habit. "I hope you are attired warmly enough."

"I assure you that I am, my lord." Lady Hallcroft, smiled up at him from beneath the brim of her plumed velvet bonnet. Her eyes sparkled like sapphires with the light of anticipation. "And if I should grow cold, I shall let you know."

Lord Hallcroft nodded, smiling again. "Then let us be off. I have our horses waiting in front." He motioned the hovering footman, who helped him into his overcoat and handed him his beaver hat, which he put on, and his crop. Then he formally offered an arm to his lady, which she took with a slight inclination of her head.

They exited through the front door of the manor house. Lord Hallcroft solicitously held on to her elbow as they walked down the icy front steps. He waved aside the groom and helped Lady Hallcroft to mount her mare himself. She enjoyed the feel of his strong hands on her waist as he tossed her up. Lady Hallcroft settled into the crafted leather sidesaddle, arranging the folds of her heavy cloak and habit skirt.

Lord Hallcroft adjusted the height of the stirrup for her. "How is that?" he asked, looking up at her.

"It's perfect, my lord, thank you," said Lady Hallcroft, giving him a bright smile. Excitement tingled inside of her, but she knew she shouldn't express an excess of emotion. His lordship's polite formality was the guideline she had taken for her own behavior. She gathered her reins in her gloved hands. "I'm ready now, my lord."

Lord Hallcroft turned and vaulted easily onto his own restive mount. He nodded to the groom, who was holding the bridles of both horses. "You may let them go, Peters. We shall not need you today."

"Very good, my lord."

Lord Hallcroft and his lady set off sedately down the graveled drive. The snow was lighter under the canopy of bare tree branches that laced overhead and the horses' hooves clopped softly on the hard-frozen surface. Soon Lord Hallcroft turned off the drive and led the way into the surrounding fallow fields. The snow was heavier on the broad expanses and had blown in white drifts against the dark hedgerows and fences.

The riders' breaths frosted on the early morning air. Lady Hallcroft drew in a deep breath, enjoying how her nose and lungs felt seared by the cold. She felt terrifically alive. It was a lovely day. As she looked around at their pale surroundings she was struck by the stark beauty. "It is wonderful!" she said, puffs of white accenting her enthusiastic exclamation.

"Yes. Look there, at how the branches of the trees are encased in ice and how their clean surfaces glisten." Lord Hallcroft pointed with his crop. "And there, at those icicles. The light catching them like that makes them sparkle like fantastic earrings of diamonds."

Lady Hallcroft agreed with her husband's assessment. She privately marveled that a gentleman as distinguished as Lord Hallcroft could take pleasure in nature's simple wonders.

She had seen how at ease he was in society and how well received he was by prominent hostesses and heads of state. Lord Hallcroft was an influential member of the House of Lords. His opinion was often sought on weighty matters and he seemed to enjoy such conversation. She was proud, of course, of his obvious intellect and the respect in which he was held.

It had not once occurred to Lady Hallcroft that her husband might also possess an appreciation of natural beauty. The new knowledge was something to be set aside and savored at a later time.

The horses' hooves were muffled by the deeper snow, so their progress was nearly noiseless. It was almost as though they were floating through the silent white landscape. Lady Hallcroft did not think she had ever seen anything half as beautiful.

When Lord Hallcroft pointed with his crop at yet another lovely sight, reminiscing about his childhood, she looked over at him with a deep affection. She thought about how much she loved him and loved to be in his company in just such a fashion. He talked with her in an open, easy manner that was at once relaxing and companionable.

She was very glad she had married him.

She had told him before that she loved him, of course, but it had always been in the sweet darkness of their bed. She wondered what he would say if she were to say the words now, and she unaccountably blushed.

Lord Hallcroft at once noticed her heightened color. "Your cheeks have turned rosy with the cold. Perhaps we should return to the manor."

"Have they? But I am not in the least chilled. Pray let us ride a bit further." Lady Hallcroft tried to master her inexplicable confusion, hoping the cold would cool her cheeks. More than anything, she didn't want the ride to end.

All at once Lord Hallcroft reached across the distance between them and caught her hand, surprising her. "You look altogether lovely, my lady."

Lady Hallcroft felt her cheeks heat again. "My lord flatters me."

"No, I promise you. I speak but the truth," said Lord Hallcroft. There was a tender light in his eyes. He looked as though he wanted to say more and she waited with bated breath.

The horses stepped aside and their clasped hands parted, ending the moment. Lady Hallcroft regretted it, for she had felt a surge of happiness at the intimate contact.

Lord Hallcroft had always been punctilious in his compliments and he always noticed if she was wearing a particularly flattering gown or hair arrangement. Yet it was the little things, like his spontaneous words just then, that made her heart sing.

She thought that he must surely love her.

He hadn't told her in so many words, but she had accepted his reticence. It was simply not in Lord Hallcroft's nature to wear his feelings on his sleeve. However, it would be very nice to hear the words spoken aloud once in a while.

Gwen had been raised in a large extended family with universal affection and she was used to exchanging endearments. It had been difficult to adjust to the more formal relationship of her marriage. But she had observed that Lord Hallcroft and his mother did not speak of their mutual devotion. Rather, it was shown in a longer handclasp or a kiss on the cheek or a solicitous word. She had assumed that was the manner in which Lord Hallcroft preferred to express his emotions and so she had adopted it for her own in order not to embarrass or disgust him.

Lady Hallcroft sighed. At such times as these, when she questioned the nuances of her marriage, she wished most to be able to confide in her mother or to solicit her father's wisdom. The lonely bits of her heart stirred. And how nice it would be to exchange confidences with her sisters and listen to her brothers' good-natured raillery.

"Are you wearied, my lady?"

Lady Hallcroft glanced over at her husband, startled out of her reflections. "Oh, no! On the contrary, it's all so beautiful and lovely that I was just thinking it is a pity we cannot share it with all of our family and friends."

Lord Hallcroft pulled up his mount and looked around him. They had ascended a slight rise and were afforded a view of several miles. Though the gray clouds were low, the atmosphere was crystal clear. Sunlight shone on the snowy landscape, limning the tree edge line of the woods, and casting a glittering net over all the world. "Yes, it is a pity indeed. This is my favorite place. I do not believe I could ever be as content anywhere else."

Lady Hallcroft looked over at him in surprise. His handsome aquiline profile was turned to her as he continued to look over the rolling lands. "But, my lord, you are an important man in the government. I would have thought that you preferred London or one of the other capitals."

Lord Hallcroft glanced around at her. A somewhat amused expression was in his eyes. "Is it so odd of me? To prefer the country?"

"Why, I suppose not," said Lady Hallcroft slowly. She, too, contemplated the view before them. A little wistfully, she said, "I would like very much to share such wonder as this with my family. It is above all things more important to me than the whirls of polite society."

"Do you miss your family, Gwen?" asked Lord Hallcroft gently.

Lady Hallcroft glanced hastily at him, then away. "Of course. But then, I am with you and so I am vastly content."

"Prettily said, my lady," said Lord Hallcroft with a smile. "Now I think we shall return to the manor. It's time that I returned you to a warm sitting room, while I must meet with my steward yet this morning."

"Very well, my lord." Lady Hallcroft stifled an instinctive protest. Obediently she turned her mare and set spur to its side. She did not understand why she should feel so bereft, but so it was.

Despite what she had just said to Lord Hallcroft, she knew that it was not quite all of the truth. Ever since they had returned to England from their bridal journey she had felt an increasing restlessness, even a discontent.

It appalled her. She was wed to the best gentleman in all of the world. How could she feel such traitorous emotions?

Lady Hallcroft didn't want to dwell on such lowering reflections. She flashed a glance at her husband even as she pressed her heel against the mare's side. "I shall race you to the trees, my lord!"

She had a glimpse of Lord Hallcroft's startled expression before her horse swept her away. Almost instantly she heard the heavy thuds of his lordship's mount behind her. Lady Hallcroft urged the mare on, laughing as the cold wind whipped her cloak into flapping dark wings. It was exhilarating to race across the snow with the thunder of hooves in her ears and the leaping of the powerful animal beneath her.

When Lord Hallcroft's heavier mount carried him past her in a swirl of snow and clods of mud, Gwen laughed again. He had already pulled up at the edge of the woods when she raced up. Her cheeks tingled with cold and she felt chilled from the slap of the wind. But none of that mattered to her as she exclaimed, "That was marvelous!"

Lord Hallcroft was grinning. His eyes glinted with shared laughter. "Yes! I didn't know you were such a hell-for-leather rider, Gwen!"

"Only wait until hunting season and I shall show you how I ride to hounds," she promised.

She shivered suddenly, uncontrollably. The exhilaration and warmth she had felt from the race were fading, leaving her more vulnerable to the cold than before.

"I don't doubt you will show us all the way, my lady. But for now let's return to the manor as quickly as possible, for I can see you are chilled through."

"I am rather," admitted Lady Hallcroft. "But it has been worth every moment."

"For me as well," said Lord Hallcroft softly. His glance and his smile were gentler than before and served to heat Gwen's heart. She stored up the memory of such things because they seemed to her so much more meaningful than the polite expressions that a gentleman such as Lord Hallcroft would naturally utter.

It was just such a glance, accompanied by words that rang with sincerity, which had first won her heart. She had been much admired and courted, so much so that she had become used to flattery. Her heart had become armored against the smooth compliments bestowed upon her by admirers, and she had learned to turn them aside.

However, Lord Hallcroft had cut through all of her defenses with one stroke when he had looked at her just so, and told her that she was adorable.

Lady Hallcroft often wondered, especially of late, where he kept that part of himself which had first inspired the spark of her love.

Chapter Two

Lord Hallcroft led the way back on what Lady Hallcroft swiftly recognized to be a straighter path to the manor than that by which they had come, so that they came into sight of the house within a few minutes. The precious time with her lord was over far too soon, but she was determined not to let her disappointment show.

They dismounted at the stables and then walked up to the house, entering it through the left wing. Lord Hallcroft held his lady's hand tucked comfortably in the crook of his elbow even after they were inside. He kept up an amusing conversation, causing Lady Hallcroft to break into a peal of laughter.

At the merry sound, a stately woman came to the door of the sitting room. She smiled at the couple. "There you are, my dears. I was informed you were out riding. How was it?"

"Cold and very, very beautiful, ma'am." Lady Hallcroft's enjoyment of the moment was effectively extinguished. She suddenly felt as though she had been caught doing something of which she should feel guilty. She gently withdrew her hand from Lord Hallcroft's arm, covering the reason behind her action by making a slight curtsy to her mother-in-law, Lady Maria.

"Good morning, Mama. I trust you slept well?" said Lord Hallcroft cheerfully.

"Exceptionally well, I assure you. Why, child, you appear to be perfectly frozen! Christopher, how can you keep Gwendolyn standing about when she is shivering so?" asked Lady Maria. She contracted her brows in an expression of concern as she looked at her daughter-in-law. "I hope you don't contract a cold, my dear."

"Oh, I am perfectly well, ma'am," said Lady Hallcroft quickly. It seemed to her that her mother-in-law was casting blame upon Lord Hallcroft. She didn't like it because Lord Hallcroft was always solicitous of her. Nor did she care for the implication that she was such a poor creature that she must naturally fall ill simply from an hour's exposure to the winter air.

"I'm sending Gwendolyn directly up to her maid to change. She became chilled only towards the last when we indulged ourselves in a race against each other," said Lord Hallcroft. He turned to his wife and lifted her gloved hand to his lips for a formal salute. His words were just as formal. "Thank you, my lady. I enjoyed our ride very much."

"It was lovely indeed." Lady Hallcroft smiled up at her husband before turning back to excuse herself to her mother-in-law. Lady Maria graciously inclined her head in acknowledgement. Lady Hallcroft turned toward the stairs, while Lord Hallcroft stepped forward to greet his mother with a kiss on the cheek which her ladyship had upturned to him.

As she ascended the stairway and turned the corner of the landing, Lady Hallcroft sighed quietly. She always felt slightly uncomfortable in her mother-in-law's presence. It was difficult to discern what Lady Maria was really thinking behind her carefully preserved expression of civility.

Lady Maria had never been unkind nor uttered a carelessly cutting remark to her daughter-in-law. But neither had her ladyship displayed the degree of warmth that Lady Hallcroft had hoped would be kindled in their relationship. It was just one of the many things Gwen wished she could talk over with her own parents and ask their advice about.

However, she was not likely to have that opportunity for any time in the foreseeable future. Lord Hallcroft had not mentioned the possibility of visiting her relations and Lady Hallcroft hesitated to bring up the subject, fearing it would sound as though she were ungrateful for the position that she had attained through her marriage.

A letter was a poor substitute when what she really wished for was a comfortable coze, with her head lying in her mother's lap.

When Lady Hallcroft had finished changing out of her habit into a blue merino-wool gown with a shawl drawn over her shoulders, she returned downstairs. She discovered without surprise that Lord Hallcroft had already closeted himself in the study with his steward. That meant she would be joining her mother-in-law in the sitting room, as she did on most days.

Lady Hallcroft sighed. She was accustomed to animated conversation and the warmth of shared hugs amongst her own family. It was still difficult for her to adjust to Lady Maria's less expressive nature.

Lady Hallcroft interpreted it as coolness towards herself, so she rather dreaded the hours she spent in Lady Maria's company. It would be particularly stifling after the invigorating morning ride she had enjoyed. Regardless of her misgivings, however, she made certain she was wearing a cheerful expression when she entered the warmth of the sitting room.

"There you are! I was beginning to wonder if you had gotten lost," said Lady Maria with a slight smile. She had looked up briefly from her darning of white household linens with her tiny exquisite stitches.

Lady Hallcroft shook her head as she crossed the room. She was a little annoyed that Lady Maria would recall the single embarrassing incident that had happened shortly after her arrival at the sprawling manor.

"I'm quite familiar with the passageways now, ma'am." She seated herself in a wingback and leaned over the arm to open the basket beside it. She drew out her embroidery piece and the silks she was working with.

"Isn't this pleasant! We're quite cozy before the fire, are we not, my dear?"

"Yes, indeed, ma'am," agreed Lady Hallcroft civilly. She bent her head over her embroidery hoop and began to draw the needle through.

Several minutes passed with only the tick of the ormolu mantle clock to mark the silence. At one point Lady Hallcroft reflected that it was a blessing she enjoyed embroidering or otherwise the time would have crawled by for her.

"It will be a beautiful altar cloth when you're finished, Gwendolyn," remarked Lady Maria.

Lady Hallcroft looked up, surprised both by the compliment and by the opening gambit of conversation. "Why, thank you, my lady. I hope to have it finished by Christmas." She waited hopefully for what else her mother-in-law might have to say.

Lady Maria merely nodded, smiled, and returned her attention to her own work. However, as Gwen quietly despaired of any further conversation, her ladyship surprised her. "I have had a delightful letter from Frances. She writes that William will be escorting her home from the seminary for the holiday."

"Indeed, ma'am? That will be a treat for all of us," said Lady Hallcroft with rising hope. Surely, with her sister-in-law and brother-in-law in residence, the days would not be as dull.

Whenever she was with Lord Hallcroft, of course, she never felt the time weighing heavily on her hands.

When she and Lord Hallcroft had been so caught up in society during the months of their journey, she had never given a thought to what her life would be like when they returned to his home. However, once at the country estate, life had become like the gentle roll of the ocean – unceasing and with no end in sight. Lady Hallcroft knew part of the fault was with her. She was used to being busy and there was very little for her to do with her time.

"Yes, indeed. It will be quite nice to have everyone gathered together under one roof again." Lady Maria was smiling slightly and as she glanced over at her daughter-in-law there was a measure of understanding in her eyes. "I suspect you in particular will enjoy having some other company besides myself during the day. You're used to having a number of people about, are you not?"

Lady Hallcroft felt herself flush. Guiltily, she wondered whether her mother-in-law was something in the way of a seer. "It's true I'm looking forward to seeing Frances and William again. We didn't have an opportunity to come to know each other very well before my lord and I embarked on our wedding journey. When are you expecting them to arrive, ma'am?"

"Oh, I expect it shall be rather sooner than later," said Lady Maria tranquilly. "Frances was always very good at dashing off a note at the last moment. I have already spoken to the housekeeper about making ready their rooms for them."

"I'm very glad your family will all be here for the holiday, my lady," said Lady Hallcroft sincerely.

"Why, thank you, Gwendolyn. And I'm glad that you have become one of us, my dear."

Taken aback by her ladyship's gracious rejoinder, Lady Hallcroft stared at her mother-in-law for several seconds until she realized how gauche she must appear. Flushing again, she bent her over her embroidery.

Chapter Three

In his study, Lord Hallcroft awaited his young wife's presence with a small crease between his dark brows. He laid his hand on the shoulder-high mantle and leaned his weight on it as he contemplated the flickering fire. His thoughts turned again to the circumstances that had led up to today's interview.

He had wed Miss Gwendolyn Harper six months before in early June. It had been a fine society wedding. He was well-known in polite society and in political circles, while Miss Harper had been one of the reigning debutantes of the Season, so their union had garnered much notice.

Theirs had been a traditional courtship. The parties had known one another's antecedents. They had met in social surroundings where their every glance and word had been scrutinized. After their betrothal was announced, their few private meetings had been correctly chaperoned. The wedding had been attended by all the pomp and ceremony their families could devise.

Lord Hallcroft had rarely been able to exchange with his betrothed more than polite, formal phrases. It had all been very correct and very dull. It was also unfortunate, since they had never established the habit of easy speech between them.

He drew his brows down as he contemplated an unpalatable fact. In the months of their marriage, he and his new bride had not made much progress in altering the stiff style of their conversation.

Lord Hallcroft's stern features softened as he remembered their first, spontaneous meeting.

She had been hurrying downstairs to return to her family's parlor, having been dispatched upon various errands before the dinner party, while he had just arrived and given his outer garments to the footman. Miss Harper's hands had been full with sundry things. In attempting to make her curtsy to him, she had dropped her fan. "Oh!"

For an instant he had wondered if she had deliberately employed a stratagem to capture his interest, but he had as quickly dismissed the ignoble thought. Miss Harper was obviously aggravated with herself, and she was also obviously uncertain what to do since she was still holding a number of other items.

He had retrieved the fan, a delicate bit of painted parchment and carved ivory sticks. It crossed his mind that the fan was a perfect foil for her quiet dark beauty. Straightening to his full height, he had presented the fan to Miss Harper with a little bow. "Allow me, ma'am." Gently, he slipped the fan between her fingers.

Miss Harper blushed. She accepted her fan with a small dignified curtsy. Raising her lovely blue eyes to his face, she said with a confiding air, "Thank you, Lord Hallcroft. It was so awkward for me, what with Mama's vinaigrette and my sister's shawl and my lovely flowers also. I couldn't quite keep hold of everything."

"Yes, I see. Perhaps I can be of further assistance. I shall take your mama's vinaigrette and your sister's shawl and carry them for you," said Lord Hallcroft, smiling down at her. He had been struck by her grace and beauty when he was first introduced to her earlier in the Season, but in that moment when all formality was dispensed with he found her to be enchanting.

"Oh, there is no need to do so," said Miss Harper, her blush deepening. "I am really not as incompetent as I must appear."

"On the contrary, I think you appear adorable," said Lord Hallcroft without thinking. As her mouth rounded in amazement, and while he wondered where that totally unpremeditated compliment had sprung from, he gently removed the items from her slackened grasp. "It's no trouble at all, you know. Now, if you will permit me, I shall escort you safely to your mother."

Miss Harper stood indecisively. She bit her lip. "But I don't really know you, my lord. I doubt it is seemly for you to carry my things."

"My lamentable manners! I am Lord Christopher Hallcroft and I am completely at your service," he said, making a courtly bow. "And you are undoubtedly someone of importance, for I find myself most anxious to serve you."

"Of course I know who you are! What I meant was, shouldn't you be properly announced?" Miss Harper cast a glance around and caught the attention of the butler.

The wooden-faced butler, who had been waiting to one side during the impromptu meeting, started forward in order to perform his duty. With a smile, Lord Hallcroft waved the man back. "I can conceive of no greater honor than for you to announce me, Miss Harper."

Miss Harper gave a small, delighted laugh. Her eyes sparkled. "I believe you are flirting shamelessly with me, my lord. I feel quite grown-up! Pray do give me escort, for I cannot find it in my heart to gainsay such a gallant gentleman."

"So I should hope," he murmured, causing her to blush again and finding that he enjoyed doing it.

After that accidental meeting, they had never been alone in one another's company until their wedding night.

Lord Hallcroft's frown deepened with his reflections. He and Lady Hallcroft had embarked immediately upon an extended wedding trip, which naturally included calling upon every society hostess in each of the European capitals they had visited. It had been interesting and very merry because the late war had ended. They had enjoyed social engagements and dissipating entertainments without equal or number in half a dozen glittering settings.

Now it was fast closing on the holiday and Lord Hallcroft felt he scarcely knew more about his lovely young bride than he had before they had been wedded. The question of what gift he could give to her had exercised his mind for some weeks, tangled as it was with a bigger question.

He was in love with Lady Hallcroft: he was perfectly certain of that. She was a lovely lady of grace and charm, warm and loving to those about whom she cared deeply. He was fairly certain she loved him. After all, she had told him so during the dark, sweet hours spent in their marital bed. However, she had not once repeated the words in daylight, outside the bedroom, and that left him with the slightest twinge of insecurity.

He strongly suspected she did not realize the depth of his feelings for her.

Lord Hallcroft had attempted to express his feelings, but even in his own ears the words he uttered were clumsy. His tongue was never facile with the pretty phrases which dropped so readily from the lips of his wife's many admirers. He sometimes envied their easy discourse. He wondered why he, a man of experience in politics, should suddenly become tongue-tied whenever he tried to expose his heart to one very dear lady.

Whenever he escorted her to a function or to the theater, Lady Hallcroft had seemed content enough to be in his company. He had no reason to complain. However, Lord Hallcroft had noticed of late, especially since their recent return to England, that his lady wife seemed unhappy. It was nothing she voiced or, indeed, anything in her attitude. There was just a look in her eyes, gone the next instant, or an occasional trick of expression, which alerted him to the disturbing fact that the woman who held his heart in her dainty hands was not content.

Lord Hallcroft was perplexed. He had given considerable thought to the matter. His imagination had supposed for him all sorts of causes. The worst of his fears he thrust brusquely aside.

As the weeks passed and the weather had grown steadily colder, he had tried to discover the reason for his wife's unhappiness. She had greeted his blunt question with an expression of amazement and dismay.

"My lord? Why, I am not unhappy. I don't know why you should ask me such." Lady Hallcroft's blue eyes were wide and incredulous.

Lord Hallcroft had hastily begged pardon and turned to an indifferent topic. But still he watched his lady. And she, made aware of his perception, had begun to behave with an unmistakable nervousness even as she showed him an all-too-eager will to please. There came to be an increasing discomfiture between the newlyweds.

Lord Hallcroft had begun to resign himself to the yawning chasm. He did not know how to bridge it. He honestly did not believe himself equal to the task of smoothing away his wife's megrims if she would not or could not confide in him.

Then he discovered what he took to be the key to his dilemma. He noticed how his wife's conversation began to turn increasingly on reminisces of her family.

It shot through him like a bolt of lightening. His relief was immense. He set aside once and for all the ignoble suspicion that Lady Hallcroft was regretting their marriage because she was wearing the willow for some unknown gentleman who rivaled Lord Hallcroft in her affections. No, Lord Hallcroft thought, Gwendolyn was not pining for another gentleman.

Lady Hallcroft was homesick for her large extended family.

Of course, the approaching Christmas holiday had much to do with it. But he suspected the problem was aggravated because he and Lady Hallcroft had not had an opportunity to establish a relationship of any depth either before or after they had wedded. Theirs was a world filled with social obligations and niceties. It was not conducive to marital communication. In short, Lord Hallcroft and his new bride were not yet comfortable with one another.

Lord Hallcroft hoped that in devising his solution to alleviate Lady Hallcroft's doldrums, he would gain a greater place in her affections. Of course, he warned himself, one never knew exactly what notion a woman might take into her head. Perhaps he was going about the business all wrong. Quite unaccountably, he felt a sense of unease.

Lord Hallcroft put a finger under the edge of his fine starched neckcloth to loosen it.

AS LADY HALLCROFT HURRIED down the hall, she wondered what was behind Lord Hallcroft's summons. He had never before sent for her to join him in his study. In fact, she had never set foot inside the room. Once she had dared to peep around the door at a time when she knew that Lord Hallcroft would be absent from the house.

She had been hesitant to enter her husband's inner sanctum because she didn't know what his reaction would have been if he were to find her there. The study was the place where Lord Hallcroft had begun to spend several hours each week, attending to all the mysterious business involved in managing a large estate. Lady Hallcroft insensibly had begun to resent the study because it represented something that took her husband away from her side.

However, now she felt only a sense of anxiety and curiosity. Halting outside the heavy door, she put up her hand to knock on one of its panels. "Enter."

Lady Hallcroft opened the door and stepped inside. She met the glance of her husband, who turned from the hearth at her entrance. "My lord? You asked for me?"

"Yes, my lady. Pray be seated." Lord Hallcroft, gestured to a wingback situated close to the fire.

Lady Hallcroft shut the door and crossed the floor, aware that Lord Hallcroft's gaze never strayed from her face. Warmth came up into her cheeks and she dropped her eyes. Seating herself, she composed her hands in her lap before she looked up at her husband. Almost hesitantly, she asked, "Have I done something to displease you, my lord?"

Lord Hallcroft looked startled. "No, of course not. Whatever gave you that idea?"

Lady Hallcroft cast down her eyes. "You have never summoned me here, to your study, my lord. I thought perhaps-"

"It wasn't my intention to make you nervous, Gwendolyn," said Lord Hallcroft. He shook his head. "Quite the opposite, actually."

She looked up at him again, puzzled. "I don't understand."

"I wish to host a Christmas party, Gwendolyn. And I wish you to handle all of the arrangements."

Lady Hallcroft was completely taken aback by surprise at his lordship's blunt announcement. Her expression must have reflected her astonishment because Lord Hallcroft immediately launched into an explanation.

"Since we've returned to England and retired here to the estate, we have not had the opportunity to entertain. I thought perhaps the holiday would be a good time for you to hostess our first large gathering." Lord Hallcroft cleared his throat. "What do you think, Gwendolyn?"

"Of course, my lord. I will be happy to take on such an agreeable task," said Lady Hallcroft quickly, anxious to please. "But-" She broke off.

"Do you have some reservation, then?"

"Yes, my lord. What of Lady Maria? Surely it's more her place to act as hostess in this house?" asked Lady Hallcroft hesitantly. "I wouldn't wish to usurp her position, my lord."

Lord Hallcroft nodded. "It is well thought of, my lady. However, you needn't concern yourself. I have already spoken to my mother and she has expressed herself delighted at the notion. In fact, her exact words were that she was delighted to be relieved of such an onerous task. She has never been particularly fond of planning large events, preferring smaller gatherings to what I have in mind."

"In that case, I shall be happy indeed to fill that office, my lord." Lady Hallcroft was thrilled. She dearly loved the holiday season and all its lovely traditions. Nothing could be more suited to give her pleasure.

Lord Hallcroft smiled. The relief was evident in his eyes. "Thank you, my lady. I'll tell the household to apply to you for all instructions."

Lady Hallcroft was warmed by his obvious approval. She knew his lordship was expressing trust in her judgment and ability. She vowed she wouldn't let him down. Curiously, she asked, "Whom shall we be inviting, my lord?"

Lord Hallcroft waved his hand. "It will be a number of people with whom I am acquainted. You needn't be concerned with that end of it. My secretary will attend to the invitations. You need only arrange for the dinner and the entertainment. In addition, I expect several of the guests will wish to extend their stay for several days."

Lady Hallcroft's heart sank. It was obvious that Lord Hallcroft had it in mind to entertain several personages from political circles. Not having been raised with such connections, she knew few from that rarified segment of society. Nor had she had an opportunity to establish more than a nodding acquaintance with any of her husband's friends before they left England on their extended wedding trip. Now she was expected to put together an elegant function for all these unknowns. She realized it was a more difficult chore that had been set before her than she had thought.

She didn't want to fail Lord Hallcroft in her first foray into entertaining. Tentatively, she asked, "My lord, might I inquire what is expected? That is, I don't know precisely how you wish me to arrange the Christmas party so that it is most pleasing to your guests."

Lord Hallcroft smiled. "Why, I think it would be best for you to arrange things just as your own family would have done at this time of the year, Gwendolyn. You've often told me in these past few weeks what cheer your family enjoyed at Christmas."

Lady Hallcroft flushed. "I apologize, my lord! I didn't realize I was boring on in such a fashion."

"Nonsense. I didn't find your reminisces boring in the least. On the contrary, I found them enlightening. I hope that in planning our own Christmas party you will be less homesick for your family," said Lord Hallcroft quietly.

Lady Hallcroft was dismayed. Her eyes flew to meet his questioning gaze. She flushed fierily. "I'm sorry. It's just that-"

Lord Hallcroft held up his hand. "You don't have to explain, Gwendolyn. I should have realized earlier how difficult it must be for you to be away from your family, especially since we have returned to England and aren't situated so very far from them."

Lady Hallcroft pressed her hands to her cheeks. "I feel so ashamed. I know I should not feel homesick! After all, I'm a married woman! I don't wish to insult you in such a fashion, my lord."

"You do not insult me, my lady," said Lord Hallcroft quietly. "It is your nature to care strongly for those for whom you have affection."

Lady Hallcroft glanced up at him, then away. "Yes," she agreed in a smothered voice.

A little diffidently, he asked, "Would it please you if we were to plan on a long visit with your family?"

She looked up again, quickly, and this time the color that rose into her face was not due to embarrassment. Her eyes suddenly sparkled with unshed tears. "Oh, Christopher! Yes, it would please me very much!"

Lord Hallcroft let out his breath in a soft sigh. He hadn't been wrong, then. He smiled down at her. "Then that's what we'll do. But first I shall ask you to direct all of your energies into our own Christmas party."

"I shall do so most willingly, my lord," said Lady Hallcroft, her fears and uncertainties fading before the glorious promise of reuniting with her beloved family.

Chapter Four

The following morning, Lady Hallcroft wakened with her thoughts already revolving upon the awesome responsibility that Lord Hallcroft had laid on her.

However, the first thing she did was to delicately ask what Lady Maria's feelings were about her taking charge of the preparations for the large gathering. Lady Hallcroft had always been careful to defer to her mother-in-law and show the proper respect for Lady Maria's authority. Even though Lord Hallcroft had assured her that all had been agreed upon, Lady Hallcroft was not so certain of her footing with Lady Maria that she was able to accept his lordship's assurance with absolute confidence. She wanted to be perfectly certain that Lady Maria indeed regarded the arrangement with complacence.

At the question, Lady Maria laughed gently and shook her head. "My dear, of course I am perfectly willing for you to make all of the arrangements. I am a very poor creature when it comes to planning for huge parties. As you must already have realized, I'm much more comfortable to leave even the mundane affairs of running this huge house in the hands of our capable staff. In fact, I have given instructions to Taylor and Mrs. Simpkins that they are to take their orders directly from you."

"Are you quite certain, ma'am?" asked Lady Hallcroft anxiously. "I don't in the least wish to put you out."

Lady Maria laid a hand on her daughter-in-law's arm. With an unwavering gaze, she said, "My dear Gwendolyn, believe me, I infinitely prefer to leave everything to you. My son has expressed his complete confidence in you and therefore I know I may rest easy."

Sensing the sincerity behind Lady Maria's words, Lady Hallcroft was able without a twinge of guilt to throw herself into devising a house party of splendid proportions. Lord Hallcroft had given her carte blanche, requesting specifically that she order all as her own family did. Recalling the wonderful Christmases of her girlhood, she began to feel a sense of excitement.

Lady Hallcroft set pen to paper, organizing her vision into a much-detailed plan. That same day she met with the butler, Taylor, and Mrs. Simpkins the housekeeper. In consultation with these worthies, Lady Hallcroft ordered massive preparations to be set in train. It wasn't long before Hallcroft Manor took on the air of a frenzied beehive.

The twelve days leading up to Christmas were the most important. The dinner menus were carefully chosen by Lady Hallcroft in consultation with the cook, but Lord Hallcroft chose the wines that would be served each evening.

Lady Maria suggested a small ball, which Lady Hallcroft interpreted to be a gently-worded command. However, she was only too glad to incorporate Lady Maria's request into her list of entertainments. It nicely rounded out her own notions of what was due Lord Hallcroft's guests.

Lady Hallcroft asked Lord Hallcroft's secretary to make arrangements for music for the ball, outlining what it was she required. She was soon informed that an orchestra, consisting of a pianoforte, a trumpet, a cello, and a violin, was engaged for the particular evening.

Lady Hallcroft saw to a few other details, too, concerning the ball, which she considered imperative. Champagne was laid in; the silver was polished; a promise was extracted from the cook that a superlative confection treat was to be provided. The carpet was rolled up out of the ballroom and the floor was scrubbed and buffed until it gleamed.

A very busy week passed, during which Lady Hallcroft saw little of her lord. She felt strangely bereft and could only be thankful she had something with which to occupy her thoughts and her time. She tried not to mind the widening gap between them. She knew that Lord Hallcroft's hours were consumed with estate matters and, lately, some political question that was the focus of lengthy correspondence.

Lady Hallcroft realized his lordship had already given instructions that the invitations for the house party to be sent out because in a very short while responses began to trickle in.

She never saw the respondents' notes, for Lord Hallcroft's secretary was quick to lay claim to them. Since Lord Hallcroft knew she was not familiar with his friends and acquaintances, she assumed his lordship preferred to leave that part of organizing the house party in the secretary's capable hands.

Lady Hallcroft didn't mind that so very much since her time was completely taken up with the rest of the preparations. However, it would have been nice to have had the opportunity to discuss with Lord Hallcroft this personage's acceptance or that individual's decline, if only to have something more to talk about.

Despite Lady Hallcroft's enjoyment of making ready for the holidays and a Christmas house party, she couldn't quite ignore the gray cloud on her horizon. There was a new lack of interaction between herself and Lord Hallcroft. They met over breakfast and dinner, but they scarcely exchanged a word otherwise. When they did converse, it was naturally over the details of the house party, which Lady Hallcroft was careful to relay to his lordship and to which he seemed to enjoy listening. However, there were no more companionable rides in the winter snow. Nor did Lord Hallcroft seem as likely to seek out her company as he once had. He seemed content to spend the evenings with both her and Lady Maria.

Lady Hallcroft could not understand it. He had once tried to spend as much time alone with her as he possibly could. The slowly gathering conviction that Lord Hallcroft was becoming slightly bored with her couldn't be set aside.

Lady Hallcroft wanted to please her husband. She thought if she did, he would naturally regard her with approval and wish to spend more time with her. It was the wish of a woman in love. The inevitable anxiety she felt over the house party and how well it would come off began to loom larger and larger in her mind.

One afternoon as Lady Hallcroft started to enter the drawing room, she heard voices and her own name. She paused behind the half-open door when her mother-in-law's voice lifted in remonstrance.

"Christopher, I cannot quite approve of this plan of yours. It's not fair to Gwendolyn."

"I know, Mama. But it is only for a short while that she will be kept in the dark. Then she will know everything."

Lady Hallcroft bit her lip, uncertain of what she should do. She did not want to enter the drawing room after such an odd conversation.

Her mind was already puzzling over the meaning of what she had heard. Should she brazen it out and pretend she hadn't heard anything or should she retreat? The decision was taken from her when the housekeeper appeared and requested her aid in settling a minor household crisis concerning the upstairs maids.

"Let us go into the library, Mrs. Simpkins. I don't wish to worry Lady Maria with such a thing," said Lady Hallcroft quietly.

"Yes, my lady."

In the process of handling the domestic issue and sending off the satisfied housekeeper, Lady Hallcroft forgot about the odd bit of overheard conversation. She didn't think of it again as she hurried off to check on the progress of one of the tasks that she had set herself for that day.

It was going on the hour before dinner when Lady Hallcroft concluded she had accomplished everything that could possibly be done that day and she went upstairs to change out of her daydress.

An hour later, having dressed for dinner, she had started downstairs when she heard Lord Hallcroft's cheerful voice drifting up from the entry hall. Lady Hallcroft glanced over the banister and saw that he was greeting two arrivals. She recognized his lordship's brother and sister and she realized that Lady Maria's sanguine observation of not many evenings past had proven true.

Lady Hallcroft hurried down the stairs to the entry hall so that she could greet her in-laws. But then she stood hovering uncertainly to one side because she didn't want to intrude too closely on what she was all too aware was an emotional moment.

It was an exuberant homecoming, with both young people throwing their arms about Lady Maria and Lord Hallcroft in turn, and talking animatedly. Observing the greetings among the family members, Lady Hallcroft was astonished. She had never seen Lady Maria display so much emotion, even wiping away a few happy tears, nor was Lord Hallcroft the least bit stiff with bear hug he was subjected to from William. He merely recommended that his younger brother be more careful of the creases in his starched neckcloth.

His brother laughed heartily. "Surely that statement is more in my line, brother!"

"You would like to think so, at any rate!" retorted Lord Hallcroft.

William Hallcroft resembled his elder brother in face and frame. He was a handsome young man, still boyishly thin but nearly as tall as Lord Hallcroft. His taste in clothing ran to dandyism and he wore his starched shirt-points ridiculously high up on his ruddy cheekbones. Lady Hallcroft smiled to herself. She thought he resembled her younger brother in manners and in fashion. She immediately felt she could be comfortable with him.

She turned her gaze upon her sister-in-law and did not feel quite so confident. There was nothing shy or retiring about Miss Hallcroft, as one would expect of such a young miss. Instead, the young lady appeared to be the epitome of fashionable élan. Lady Hallcroft felt certain that Miss Hallcroft would never feel a second's anxiety about presiding over a house party consisting of influential individuals in government.

Lord Hallcroft's sister was a petite blonde with a curling mop of hair, speaking eyes, and a pert nose and mouth. Miss Frances Hallcroft was a veritable whirlwind of energy and there could be no more striking contrast than between her animated countenance, coupled with quick-silver movements, and Lady Maria's studied elegance.

Frances had already peeled off her kid gloves and was now undoing the ribbons of her fashionable bonnet, which she immediately pulled off of her head. She handed her possessions to the maid who stood a little to one side of her. "Whew! That's better."

"But what have you done to your hair, Frances?" asked Lady Maria, eyeing her daughter's short coiffure askance.

"I had it cropped. It's all the crack," said Frances, fluffing her curls with her long slender fingers. "Do you like it?"

"I am not certain that I do," said Lady Maria judiciously with a faint frown.

"Oh, Mama!" Frances giggled and shook her head with a tolerant, worldly air. "I assure you, it simply wasn't possible to keep my past style! Why, I would look a perfect quiz!"

Lady Hallcroft realized that her fingertips were touching her own longer arrangement of cascading curls and she hastily dropped her hand. She felt all sorts of fool to have betrayed herself. She hoped that no one had noticed her unconscious movement.

"I suspect you'll turn quite a few heads with such a modish look," said Lord Hallcroft dryly.

Frances's dimples peeped out on either side of her mobile mouth. "So I should hope!" Her eyes traveled past her brother's figure and settled on the hovering lady of the house. "Oh!"

Lord Hallcroft, following his sister's gaze, appeared to notice his wife's presence for the first time. "Gwen, you have met my brother, William, and my reprehensible sister, Frances," he said, turning toward his wife and holding out his hand to her. With a firm clasp on her fingers, he drew her forward into the circle.

"Yes, of course. How do you do? I'm happy you have come," said Lady Hallcroft politely, smiling at them. She was anxious that she make a good impression because, as she had once remarked to Lord Hallcroft, it was important to her to be well-liked by all of his family and friends. Of course, even after several weeks she still wasn't certain that Lady Maria really liked her. Lady Hallcroft hoped her relationship with these younger members might be easier to establish, especially since they seemed to be more like her in their outward expressions of affection.

"Well! You come in very good time, my dears. You must go up immediately to put off your traveling things, for we are about to sit down to dinner," said Lady Maria, smiling at her younger children.

William rubbed his hands together. "Dinner! I shall not be many minutes, I assure you!" With a bow in Lady Hallcroft's direction he bounded up the stairs.

Lord Hallcroft laughed. "Will hasn't changed a bit. He still eats like a horse."

"Yes; I don't know where he puts it," said Frances, shaking her head. She reached up on tiptoe to brush a kiss against her older brother's cheek. "I shall only be a quarter hour, I promise." She also ran up the stairs, followed more slowly by her faithful maid.

Lady Hallcroft beckoned the butler to her side and quietly instructed him. "Taylor, pray inform the cook to set dinner back."

The butler nodded and exited the entry hall.

Lord Hallcroft smiled at his wife and his mother. "We have cause to celebrate this evening, ladies. May I escort you both into the parlor where we shall await our two returned sojourners?"

"Indeed you may, Christopher. I'm anxious to hear everything that William and Frances have to tell us," said Lady Maria, accepting her son's escort and tucking her hand inside his elbow.

Lady Hallcroft took her husband's proffered arm. She smiled up at him. "I'm happy your brother and sister have arrived in such good time, my lord. It will make the holidays that much more enjoyable."

"I'm certain of it," murmured Lord Hallcroft with a smile.

Chapter Five

All the talk was for the upcoming house party. Frances had initially bemoaned the fact that she was not to enjoy the society of her own friends during the house party; but after a short interview with Lord Hallcroft behind the closed doors of the study, she suddenly stopped voicing her disappointment.

Lady Hallcroft felt sorry for her sister-in-law, interpreting the change to mean that Lord Hallcroft had sternly remonstrated with his sister. She therefore went out of her way to include Frances in her activities and to ask her advice on various things, so that a good understanding seemed to be developing between them.

As for the younger son of the house, William expressed himself fully satisfied with whatever preparations were being made. "I'm just jolly glad to be home. There is the duck hunting and all sorts of sport to be had and meat pies and such to look forward to," he said.

William liked the decorative fir garlands and red ribbons that had gone up, but it was the tantalizing scents of roasted goose and Christmas puddings that began wafting through the house that he most approved. He was seen more than once with his nose lifted high, sniffing appreciatively in a manner much akin to that of the hounds that were always following close at his heels.

Lady Maria was gracious enough to tell her daughter-in-law that the manor house had never appeared more handsome than bedecked in its fragrant greenery, red bows, and tinsel. Lady Hallcroft glowed with the praise and she felt for the first time that perhaps Lady Maria did indeed approve of her. When Lord Hallcroft echoed his mother's sentiments, Gwen felt herself to be quite in charity with everyone.

Everywhere one looked, there was the scent and sight of Christmas. Fir decorated the mantels in every room and was wound through the banister and up to the upper balcony. For days the sideboards had groaned with the scrumptious offerings from the kitchen – roasted fowl, hams, puddings, pasties, sweetmeats and pies. The heady scents of the traditional eggnog and rum punch hung on the air. Everything that Lady Hallcroft could possibly think of to make the holiday more festive had been set in motion. She anxiously hoped that Lord Hallcroft's guests would not despise her efforts.

Lady Hallcroft still fretted over her first attempt to entertain for Lord Hallcroft's set and hoped for success. When she asked Lord Hallcroft more specifically when he expected the guests to arrive, he was vague. She was forced to conclude that it was an unimportant detail to his lordship. However, it was of vital significance to her. She gave standing orders to the housekeeper to keep all the bedrooms in a ready state so that at any given moment guests could step into them and feel immediately at home.

Despite her insecurity, Lady Hallcroft was also feeling a keen sense of excitement. The Christmas holiday had always been one of her favorite times of the year and it had always connoted warmth and affection and family. She had written to her parents to convey an open invitation to them and any other members of her family who might wish to visit. When a letter arrived, addressed to her in a beloved, familiar handwriting, Gwen opened it eagerly. Her sense of joy was dimmed when she read her mother's disappointing reply.

She unconsciously made a sound of dismay, which her sister-in-law was quick to hear. Frances looked up from the ladies' magazine that she was perusing. "Have you received bad news, Gwen?"

"Not bad, precisely, but certainly unexpected," said Lady Hallcroft. She looked up from her mother's closely written sheets and managed to put a credible smile in place. "It seems that my parents have made other arrangements already for the holidays, so they have declined my invitation to visit us."

"I shouldn't mind it, Gwen, for my brother has made plans for the holidays that must meet with your approval," said Frances offhandedly.

"Whatever do you mean? We're having this house party, certainly, but is there something else of which I'm not yet aware?"

Flushing, Frances just stared at her sister-in-law. Gwen suddenly realized that the younger woman was looking strangely guilty. Before she could pursue her question, Frances scrambled up, allowing the magazine to fall to the floor. "Excuse me, I'm certain I hear my mother calling to me."

"Frances, pray tell me! Is there something I should know?" asked Lady Hallcroft, feeling the beginning of alarm.

Frances's usual self-possession appeared to have deserted her. "Oh, I've said too much already! Pray forgive me! And pray, pray don't tell Christopher that I have!"

With that, Frances whirled away and left the parlor, leaving Lady Hallcroft staring after her in lively surprise. Eventually it occurred to Gwen that she had been unpleasantly left in the dark, and that realization brought to her recollection the tidbit of conversation she had overheard between Lady Maria and Lord Hallcroft.

She couldn't imagine what sort of plans Lord Hallcroft could have made, or even that there would be time to fit anything else into the holiday season, besides the house party and the visit to her family.

The more she turned it over in her mind, the more logical became a very unpleasant conclusion. It appeared to her that Lord Hallcroft had apparently forgotten his solemn promise that she could visit with her family after the house party. Little by little, as she reflected upon her conversation with her sister-in-law, she grew angrier and angrier.

Lady Hallcroft abruptly left the parlor and went upstairs to her bedroom, ordering her maid to deny her to anyone because she was laid down with a headache.

She spent the remainder of the afternoon in her bedroom. More than once she started to go down to Lord Hallcroft's study and request a private audience with him. However, in the end she decided against such a confrontation. It could only serve to anger Lord Hallcroft and she didn't feel so secure in his lordship's affections that she felt able to brave either his wrath or his rejection.

The hours Gwen spent alone in her bedroom didn't bring her good counsel. After much reflection, she decided there was little she could do except pretend that she was still in total ignorance of Lord Hallcroft's perfidy.

She could not overcome the hurt she felt that Lord Hallcroft apparently intended to break his word to her. Even more than the lost opportunity to visit with her family was the inescapable feeling that all Christmas cheer had been sucked out of her.

Lady Hallcroft shed a few tears; but then, with the striking of the hour by the hall clock, she dried her face and rang for her maid, to make herself presentable for dinner. Then she slowly went downstairs.

Lady Hallcroft crossed the hall to join the rest of the household in the parlor before dinner. She paused in the doorway and glanced around. Here, too, the signs of the holiday were lavishly displayed. A kissing bough hung from the chandelier in the parlor, heavily laden with bright red apples and candies and tiny gifts and candles. Mistletoe, lavishly beribboned, garnished the center of the bough.

The kissing bough was particularly hard to look at. It was unfortunate she would not herself ever be the object of sweet gallantries under that same bough.

Lady Hallcroft suppressed the traitorous thought at once. It was simply not in Lord Hallcroft's nature to be overly demonstrative. Besides, she wasn't feeling particularly kindly toward her husband just then and she would almost certainly have rebuffed any such overture from him.

Gwen quietly greeted Lady Maria and Frances with a smile and a gracious word as she made her way across the room. Ignoring Frances' swift speculative glance, she took her place in a wingback before the blazing hearth.

"How are you, Gwendolyn? I understand you suffered from the headache this afternoon," said Lady Maria.

"I'm much better now, my lady." Lady Hallcroft was aware of her sister-in-law's stare and lifted her gaze to the young woman, holding the glance steadily. Frances was the first to look away, a slight flush rising in her face.

Lady Hallcroft calmly took out her embroidery and began adding delicate stitches to the exquisite design on the altar cloth. She listened with only half an ear to the conversation between Frances and Lady Maria, responding as necessary when she was addressed. Otherwise she took no part in what was going forward, preferring her own thoughts to her companions' discourse.

At some point Lord Hallcroft and William entered the parlor, animatedly discussing a recent bout of billiards. Lady Hallcroft glanced up briefly, without forethought, to look at her husband. Upon meeting his smiling expression, she forced a tiny smile to her face. However, inside she was seething with resentment and hurt. She dropped her eyes and applied herself to her embroidery, using her handiwork as a shield against being drawn completely into conversation.

When it was time to go in to dinner, Lady Hallcroft rose gracefully to her feet and accompanied her husband and his family into the dining room. It was the longest meal she had ever partaken of and she was thankful when it was over.

There was an unusual heaviness of spirit plaguing her and she was glad to return to the drawing room with the two other ladies. The gentlemen would naturally rejoin them after they had finished their after-dinner wine, and coffee would then be served. Lady Hallcroft settled down again with her embroidery and wished passionately that the unfortunate evening would pass quickly so she could go upstairs to bed.

Lord Hallcroft and William returned. Lady Hallcroft acknowledged their presence with a smile and a nod, but she didn't make any attempt to put herself forward. Once again she used her embroidery as an excuse to distance herself.

Her reflections were somber. She wondered when she could visit her family. It must be sometime after the holiday, of course. She tried to make some plans, but her thoughts perversely wandered and settled onto Lord Hallcroft.

Chapter Six

The clock on the mantel struck the hour, startling Lady Hallcroft from her reverie. She heard the murmur of conversation, the occasional rise of laughter. The warmth of hearth and family were all around her, but she felt it merely pointed up her loneliness.

She didn't understand her husband. She didn't really feel she was one of the Hallcroft household. Despite all she had accomplished in making Hallcroft Manor reflective of the season, she felt separated from the joyous spirit of Christmas.

Lady Hallcroft suddenly yearned for her own family. She was assured of her place in their affection. Tears stung her eyes. She blinked them back so she could see the flash of her needle.

Lord Hallcroft had more than once glanced in his wife's direction. She had been oblivious of his observation. He rose from his seat to approach her. "It's the first of the twelve nights. We'll light the first candle soon. May I interest you in helping me with that traditional task, my lady?"

Lady Hallcroft's heart twisted with pain. She thought she could stand no more. She stabbed her needle into the fabric and rolled up the embroidery. Exercising self-control, when what she really wished to do was snap at him, she said quietly, "Forgive me, my lord. I'm not feeling well and I have been thinking that I should like to go up early to my room."

"Poor Gwendolyn had the headache earlier this afternoon, Christopher. You must try to get her to rest, for I suspect she has been going the pace too fast," said Lady Maria, apparently overhearing something of their conversation.

Lord Hallcroft looked down at his wife, concerned. He hadn't noticed before, but she did look to be a little under the weather. Certainly her generally sunny disposition had been rather subdued that evening. "I'm sorry to hear you are in distress, my lady."

"Are you? Are you really?" asked Lady Hallcroft hastily, under her breath. Her bosom was heaving with her repressed feelings. Her eyes flashed as she jumped to her feet. She managed to keep her voice low enough that it did not carry to the others. "It's strange, then, that you've made it impossible for me to be aught else! When you *promised* me that I should visit with my family!"

Lady Hallcroft felt she had to get away or otherwise she would probably say something she would truly regret. She turned abruptly, but before she could make good her escape she was caught fast by the elbow. She looked up, astonished that Lord Hallcroft would detain her. She was even more surprised by the grimness of his expression.

"My lord!" She directed a meaningful glance down at his long fingers which were clasped about her forearm.

"I apologize for my heavy-handedness, my lady. However, I should like to hear what it is that has offended you so," said Lord Hallcroft. He gestured courteously with his free hand, as though requesting her company, but the pressure of his fingers left little doubt in Gwen's mind that he was quite determined that she accompany him.

Lady Hallcroft threw another glance up at his profile when she realized that he was inexorably drawing her over to the settee set against the wall. They were not even to go into a separate room, but would have this conversation with his family seated at the far end of the parlor. Humiliation suffused her; it did not occur to her that there would have been a great deal of speculation among his family if she and Lord Hallcroft were to precipitously desert the parlor.

"Pray be seated, my lady."

Lady Hallcroft sat down, perforce because she didn't wish to make any more of a scene, but she sat bolt upright with her hands held tight in her lap. Her eyes lowered, she said, "I do not wish to discuss this matter with you, my lord."

"Nevertheless, my lady, you may begin with your reference to your family. That is apparently the crux," he said quietly.

Lady Hallcroft rounded on him, stung out of her dignified demeanor by his reasonable tone. "How could it be otherwise, my lord? At a passing remark from myself that I should like to see my family at Christmas, your sister tells me that you've made other plans for the entire holiday season! Then Frances looked all shades of guilty and begged me not to reveal that she had said anything."

Lord Hallcroft regarded her with the dawn of understanding, which became swiftly intermingled with amusement. "Gwendolyn, I assure you that's not quite the way things are."

Lady Hallcroft was further incensed by the springing of laughter into his eyes. The hurt she felt intensified. "Oh, naturally not! I imagine Frances was simply rattling away in her inimitable style and there is not a particle of truth in it!"

Lord Hallcroft had the audacity to laugh.

Lady Hallcroft rose hastily from the settee. "Excuse me, my lord. I mustn't neglect my duties. Lady Maria will wish me to pour the coffee!"

She swept past him, her head held high. Her wrist was caught in a gentle yet commanding grasp. Gwen was consternated as she turned to face her husband. More and more Lord Hallcroft was surprising her, throwing her increasingly off balance. He had never before used his stronger physicality with her. "Unhand me!"

"I don't think so, my lady. You have misinterpreted my meaning."

Lady Maria interrupted. "Christopher, it's time to light the first candle on the kissing bough. Pray do come do the honors."

Glancing briefly in Lady Maria's direction, Lord Hallcroft stood indecisively. He wanted to finish the discussion with his wife. He could scarcely believe that such a quarrel had flared up between them. Indeed, he was more than a little surprised that his meek and biddable wife could be staring up at him with such a challenge sparkling in her blue eyes. In the end, the decision was wrested from him as Lady Hallcroft took advantage of his slackened grasp and freed herself with a quick yank.

Lord Hallcroft watched as his wife walked swiftly away, crossing the parlor with an angry sway to her skirts. He saw that Lady Maria, as well as his brother and sister, were beginning to realize that something untoward had taken place. All were eyeing Lady Hallcroft's averted face before swiftly glancing at his darkened expression.

Lord Hallcroft knew he was scowling. He made an effort to rid himself of his frown. Unless he wished to initiate an embarrassing scene, he had no alternative but to pretend that there was nothing amiss. "I shall be happy to do the honors, Mama."

Lord Hallcroft ignored the expressions of relief on all of their faces. He walked over to take the brand that the butler ceremoniously offered to him. He lifted the flame and solemnly lit the first of the twelve candles which symbolized the twelve days of Christmas.

Upon the candle catching fire, Frances laughed and clapped her hands and William whooped. "Now let's sing some of the old carols!" exclaimed Frances, her eyes bright.

"Oh, let's do, by Jove! How jolly! Mama, will you play for us?" asked William.

"Of course I shall, my dears." Lady Maria sat down at once at the pianoforte. She began to play one of the joyous traditional songs and her two younger children loudly sang along. They were all studiously ignoring Lady Hallcroft, who hadn't volunteered to join them but instead had turned her back.

Lord Hallcroft reluctantly lifted his voice as well. Though he had never felt less like it, he was aware that if he did not participate there would be questions from his family that he might find difficult to answer.

He glanced over at Lady Hallcroft. She was standing at one of the tall windows, one hand holding back the heavy drapery as she gazed through the glazed panes. There was a forlorn air in her posture that made him want to go to her, but he suspected she would not welcome his intrusion into her privacy.

For the next hour, Lord Hallcroft took note that his lady wife was careful to avoid his gaze. After the caroling, she served coffee and even when she handed a cup to him, she did not meet his eyes. Then she initiated a game of charades with his brother and sister, which kept all three thoroughly entertained and did much to dissipate the previously uncomfortable atmosphere. Urged at first by his sister to join in the simple entertainment, Lord Hallcroft declined. He was certain, judging from Lady Hallcroft's sudden tenseness of figure, that his participation would have been a detriment to her amusement.

It gave him a distinctly hollow feeling that his young wife, whom he adored, did not wish to have anything to do with him that evening. He had badly misjudged in his dealings with her. That was abundantly clear to him.

LADY HALLCROFT STARED up into the bed canopy above her head. The long unhappy evening had finally ended and she had been able to escape to her apartment. The only consolation she had taken with her was that the onset of the scene between herself and Lord Hallcroft had been brushed through well enough. She'd dreaded queries from the family and she'd been thankful that they had desisted.

Gwen had half-hoped, half-feared, Lord Hallcroft would follow her. But he had not. She assured herself it was for the best. She turned on her side, tucking her hand between her cheek and the down-filled pillow. She should feel better than she did, she thought forlornly. She'd had the courage to stand up to him.

However, nothing she told herself could erase the hollow feeling inside of her. She and Lord Hallcroft had never quarreled before.

The brocaded bed curtains could be drawn at night to protect the sleeper from the drafts, but Gwen usually left one curtain partly open so she could see the fire if it was still burning. This night, shadows from the firelight played over the rosettes and vines carved into the headboard.

A small table beside the bed held a candle and flint. Her books were tumbled across the tabletop. She had read for a short time before snuffing the candle and sliding under the covers. She had still hoped that her husband would come to her after giving her time to ready herself for bed. But as the minutes ticked by, she had realized that Lord Hallcroft was not coming.

The worst thing was that after she had voiced her suspicion that he meant to break his word to her, she had instinctively felt an inner denial that he would actually do such a thing. It would have relieved her mind greatly to find out the truth.

Lady Hallcroft brushed a tear from her cheek. She could not sleep for thinking back over their quarrel. Finally, she concluded that it was easier simply to get up than to lie tossing and turning, feeling miserable and angry by turns. She reached out for the flint and lit her candle. The bedroom lightened, long shadows flickering across the walls.

Lady Hallcroft threw back the bedclothes and reached for her wrapper. She didn't want any of the books she already had. None of them had engaged her mind enough that she could stop thinking about the quarrel that had sprung up between herself and Lord Hallcroft. She decided she would go downstairs to the library and find another book to read. She belted the robe tightly around her small waist.

Shielding her candle flame with her cupped palm, Lady Hallcroft cautiously eased open the door, hardly daring to breathe when it softly creaked. The darkened house remained quiet. She sped swiftly down the hall, her bare feet soundless on the carpet.

On the stairs, she moved more cautiously with one hand on the smooth banister as she felt her way down. Suddenly, a stair creaked loudly underfoot. She froze instinctively, her heart pounding. Straining her ears, she could detect nothing out of the ordinary disturbing the silent dark.

It suddenly struck her as amusing that she was reacting much as a housebreaker might, and on a breathless laugh she continued her descent. At the bottom of the stairs she turned, the candlelight flickering with the passage of air. She traversed the deserted great hall and walked quickly to the double doors of the library. Soundlessly she turned the knob and went into the darkened room, holding her candle high.

Moonlight filtered through a part in the drawn draperies so that even without her candle Lady Hallcroft would have had no difficulty in making out the placement of the furniture. A massive oak library table dominated the center of the room. Chairs of a bygone age, with wooden arms and carved backs and red velvet cushions, were placed around the table. Without needing to look, Lady Hallcroft knew the walls were covered with floor-to-ceiling bookshelves, interspersed at intervals with several gilt-framed portraits of ancestors. The bust of a grim-faced predecessor stood in one darkened corner.

Lady Hallcroft set her flickering candle on the library table. The shadows danced and something seemed to flicker across the bust. She looked quickly towards the still-dark corner, her heart thumping a little, but she saw nothing untoward.

Then as her gaze became more focused, she perceived the figure of a man in shirt and breeches watching her from the shadows of the room. He was near the door that gave directly onto Lord Hallcroft's study. Lady Hallcroft gave a frightened gasp and started to turn, to run.

The man moved swiftly. With two bounds he was beside her. A hard palm clamped over her mouth, stifling the scream that rose in her throat. He yanked her back against him, pinning her against him with his hard arms. "Softly, sweetheart. You don't want to raise the house."

Recognizing the low voice, Gwen gave a sob and ceased struggling. Immediately the hand came away from her mouth and she was turned in the loosened circle of arms so that she was folded close against Lord Hallcroft's chest. She reached up to clutch his shirt-front. "You frightened me horribly," she whispered. "I thought you were a housebreaker."

"What are you doing down here, Gwen?" asked Lord Hallcroft.

"I-I couldn't sleep," said Lady Hallcroft, laying her head against his strong shoulder. She closed her eyes, a trickling tear escaping from under her lids.

His breath stirred her hair as he sighed. "Nor I. My guilty conscience wouldn't give me leave."

"I'm sorry, my lord. I should not have behaved so childishly," said Lady Hallcroft in a low voice.

"No, don't apologize. I should have realized how it must have sounded to you," said Lord Hallcroft. He set her back from him a little so that he could look down into her pale face. "Gwen, I swear I shall not renege on my promise to you. You shall be allowed to spend time with your beloved family."

Lady Hallcroft shook her head. "But that's just it, my lord! That's why I feel so low. I know you would never break your word. How could I have doubted you, even for a second?"

Lord Hallcroft eased her securely back into his arms. The hard warmth of his body was comforting. "We made a misstep, Gwen. We don't know one another very well, it seems. But I should like to know you better."

It was Lady Hallcroft's turn to pull back, though she still stayed close within the circle of his arms. "I wish to know you better, too."

"Then let's make a pact, my lady. We must give voice to our feelings and our thoughts to each other," said Lord Hallcroft.

Lady Hallcroft eyed him uncertainly. "Do you *truly wish* me to do that, my lord?"

"Indeed I do," he said firmly.

"Then pray take me back to bed, Christopher," said Lady Hallcroft in a breathy voice, feeling very daring.

Lord Hallcroft drew in his breath. "I shall be happy to do so," he said, his voice suddenly husky with feeling. He swept her up into his arms and strode swiftly out of the library.

Chapter Seven

The well-sprung carriage rocked in a soothing rhythm. The cold of winter was outside, but Lady Hallcroft was perfectly comfortable. She had a heavy lap rug tucked snugly over her legs and a heated brick to warm her feet. Lord Hallcroft sat beside her.

The night of their quarrel had ended much better than Lady Hallcroft had anticipated, and they had also talked of many things. Her lonely heart had been soothed by his lordship's tenderness. She was happier than she would ever have thought possible only days before.

However, Lady Hallcroft was restive now. She finally admitted to herself the reason. She was uncertain of her reception at their journey's end. An aged female relative, Lady Eagleton, hadn't been able to attend their wedding. Lord Hallcroft told her that it was his duty to introduce her to the old lady.

When William and Frances learned that Lord Hallcroft meant to take his new bride to meet their aged aunt, they had both expressed amazed horror.

"I shouldn't like to be in your shoes, Gwen," said Frances with an artistic shudder.

"No, indeed! The old lady gives me a fright every time I see her," agreed William.

"It's very proper for Gwendolyn to make your aunt's acquaintance. Aunt Sophronia was ill at the time of the wedding, you will recall, and could not attend," said Lady Maria reprovingly.

"Are you going, Mama?" asked William pointedly.

Lady Maria had looked taken aback and even somewhat alarmed by the suggestion. "Why, no, I don't think so."

With a nod, William turned to Gwen. "You see? My brother is the only one that the old lady doesn't intimidate. Even Mama prefers to steer wide of Aunt Sophronia."

"Oh dear," murmured Lady Hallcroft.

"Precisely," said Frances with another sympathetic glance.

Now thinking back on that conversation, Lady Hallcroft made a slight face. It did not ease her insecurity over the upcoming visit that Lord Hallcroft appeared to have sunk into a deep reverie. Even though they had aired the misunderstanding between them, Lady Hallcroft was hesitant to break into her husband's thoughts by engaging him in conversation. She gave herself over to the changing landscape outside the glazed window.

The journey was quickly over and the carriage drew up to an ivy-covered manor house. The front door opened and a footman ran quickly down the steps to open the carriage door and hand out the guests. Lord Hallcroft and his lady trod up the shallow stone steps and entered the house, where their outer wraps were taken by another footman.

"I shall announce you, my lord," said the butler, and went away with a stately tread.

Lord Hallcroft smiled down reassuringly at his wife. "You'll like my aunt, I assure you."

"I'm certain I shall, my lord," responded Lady Hallcroft with an answering smile, but she still felt some inner trepidation. After all, she'd heard quite a lot about Lady Eagleton from the young Hallcrofts.

The butler returned to lead them to Lady Eagleton and Lady Hallcroft took a deep sustaining breath. Lord Hallcroft offered his arm. He smiled encouragingly down at her. She lifted her head and placed her hand on his forearm, glad for his escort.

When they were ushered into the parlor, Lady Hallcroft knew her fears were justified. Lady Eagleton was seated on a settee with three of her lapdogs. The lady's sharp eyes were narrowed on the handsome couple that approached her. Lady Hallcroft felt raked by the lady's razor-sharp glance, which assessed and dismissed her in one and the same moment. She tightened her fingers on Lord Hallcroft's arm.

Lady Eagleton extended her hand toward Lord Hallcroft. She was smiling slightly, which served to relax her stern features. "Well, nephew?

Have you nothing to say for yourself? It's about time that you saw fit to visit me."

Lord Hallcroft gave a laugh. He took his aunt's hand and kissed her gnarled knuckles. "I knew you would give me a scold, Aunt Sophronia."

"As well you might. Rumor has it you returned to England weeks past. I take it in bad part I haven't seen you before this! But then, your time has been otherwise engaged," said Lady Eagleton, turning her gaze again to the lady on her nephew's arm. "Pray introduce me, Christopher."

"Allow me to present my wife, Lady Gwendolyn Hallcroft," said Lord Hallcroft. He pressed his wife's fingers in a reassuring fashion before he drew her forward.

The two ladies exchanged polite greetings. Lady Eagleton pushed two of her lapdogs off of the settee, keeping just the one that remained on her lap. "Sit beside me, Lady Hallcroft," she commanded.

Lady Hallcroft did as she was bid, throwing a wondering glance at Lord Hallcroft as she did so. He looked amused, which served to bolster her confidence. She trusted that Lord Hallcroft wouldn't throw her to the wolves, or in this case, the she-wolf. "I'm happy to do so, my lady," she said civilly.

"Oho, you are, are you? Aren't you afraid of me, girl?" demanded Lady Eagleton, directing a fierce stare at her.

"To be sure, I've heard of your formidable reputation, my lady. But my lord holds you in high esteem and I trust in his judgment," said Lady Hallcroft steadily.

She was discomfited by the lady's high-handed manner, which bordered on rudeness, but she thought she knew better than to allow discomfort to show. Her instinct was proven to be correct when Lord Hallcroft chuckled. "Bravo, my lady. You've quite taken the wind out of her ladyship's sails."

Lady Eagleton snorted, but she appeared pleased. "At least you're not a puling miss, as so many of the young women are these days. I can't abide mousey women who jump at their own shadows."

"Quite. But you do like them to turn pale with fear at receiving one of your basilisk stares," said Lord Hallcroft. He seated himself in a wingchair facing the settee, crossed his legs, gently swinging one booted foot.

Lady Eagleton showed her teeth.

Lady Hallcroft assumed that her ladyship was expressing her amusement, an impression borne out by Lady Eagleton's next comment.

"I've always liked you , Christopher. You make me laugh." Lady Eagleton turned to her seat companion. "Now tell me about yourself, Lady Hallcroft."

"I don't know that there is much to tell," said Lady Hallcroft, taken aback.

"Of course there is. You're a person, aren't you? You have talents and dreams, don't you? Tell me about your wedding journey. Where did you go? Whom did you meet?"

Lady Hallcroft threw a helpless glance toward Lord Hallcroft. She was embarrassed to be made the center of attention by the extraordinary old woman. But Lord Hallcroft gave the faintest of nods, as though he was perfectly at ease with his aunt's odd humor.

Little by little, Lady Eagleton drew out of Lady Hallcroft her impressions and observations about the six-month-long tour of the Continent, her efforts aided by Lord Hallcroft's contributions. As the two together recalled certain happenings and shared their mutual amusement in glances and smiles, Gwen began to realize just what a magical time it had been. She realized she would always remember her wedding journey with Lord Hallcroft as one of the best of possible times.

Lady Eagleton was adept at extracting information. Lady Hallcroft didn't know when or how it happened, but at some point she began to relate anecdotes about her family. Upon the realization, she abruptly broke off in confusion. "Forgive me, my lady. I didn't mean to bore on in such a fashion."

"Nonsense! I'm perfectly entertained."

"However, I realize that you cannot possibly be more than politely interested in personages you have never met."

"As you will, Lady Hallcroft," said Lady Eagleton with a dismissive shrug.

Tea was served and it was a large, elaborate affair with plum cake and biscuits and fruits, but Lady Hallcroft scarcely noticed because Lady Eagleton began to reminisce about her own travel experiences. It seemed that in her heyday, Lord and Lady Eagleton had been inveterate travelers, and they had been as far afield as the Levant and Egypt. Lady Hallcroft sat rapt, listening while her hostess spun magic tales of camels and shipwreck and vast pyramids.

At last, when Lady Eagleton observed her voice was becoming hoarse from all of her storytelling, Lady Hallcroft sighed in contentment. She didn't know when her fear of Lady Eagleton had left her and become admiration. "How I envy you, my lady. You make it all sound so very exciting."

"Indeed it was. I'm glad I did it, so that I have the memories. Now, I don't get around as well as I once did and it would be impossible for me to do even a portion of what we once accomplished," said Lady Eagleton. She pointed a boney forefinger. "I shall end with a bit of advice to you, Lady Hallcroft. Take pleasure in life as much as you are able. Then you will have few regrets."

"I never knew you to be a philosopher, ma'am," said Lord Hallcroft with a grin.

Lady Eagleton gave a rusty chuckle. "I'm not. I am merely an old woman with a vast amount of experience behind me." She gave an abrupt nod. "I shall tell you this, too, both of you. Don't allow convention or other people's opinions to dictate how you shall live, but instead be true to God and to yourselves."

"I shall remember all of it, my lady," promised Lady Hallcroft, taking it all to heart.

"See that you do," said Lady Eagleton. She reached over to briefly press the young woman's hand. "I've enjoyed our visit tremendously, my dear. I hope you will return."

"I would like that, my lady," said Lady Hallcroft with sincerity. It was odd. She had begun by being intimidated by Lady Eagleton, but now she liked her ladyship very well. Lady Eagleton's manners might be unfashionably abrupt, even rude, but her ladyship was obviously a woman of character.

She saw that Lord Hallcroft had risen and she also got to her feet, realizing they were ending their visit.

Lord Hallcroft took a cordial leave of his aunt and waited while the ladies exchanged civilities before he escorted his lady out to their carriage.

After they had seated themselves and the carriage door was shut, Lord Hallcroft asked curiously, "Well, was my aunt as bad as Will and Frances led you to believe?"

"Indeed! Lady Eagleton was every bit as frightening as she was painted," said Lady Hallcroft, nodding. She thought she had been too forthcoming and hastened to add, "However, by the end of our visit I could quite see how you could hold her in great affection, my lord. Lady Eagleton is a fascinating woman and I thought that she was very gracious to me. I cannot imagine that she found my own stories to be particularly interesting but not once did she indicate her boredom."

"I don't think my aunt was bored. On the contrary, I believe she was quite taken with you, my lady."

Lady Hallcroft grew pink with gratification. "I do hope so, my lord. It must be an object with me to make myself agreeable to any member of your family."

"The wife I have chosen is approved by those whose opinions matter the most to me," said Lord Hallcroft. "Can you doubt it, Gwen?"

Lady Hallcroft shook her head, wrinkling her brows. "Sometimes I do, my lord. Sometimes I feel as though I am living in a dream and one day I shall awaken."

"I trust it is a pleasant dream, my lady," said Lord Hallcroft softly, glancing down into her face.

"So it is, my lord," said Lady Hallcroft, smiling at him with a sideways glance. She was recalling details from the night before. It would be wonderful were she and Lord Hallcroft able always to be in such agreement. Perhaps as she learned better how to relate to Lord Hallcroft's family, she and Lord Hallcroft would also become better companions to one another. Certainly she hoped that they would deal as famously together as Lady Eagleton and her lord had done.

"What are you thinking about now, my lady?"

Lady Hallcroft tucked her hand into the crook of Lord Hallcroft's elbow. She looked up with a confiding smile. "Only that I hope we shall be able to look back on our lives and be satisfied that we dealt well with one another, my lord."

Lord Hallcroft was astonished. He hadn't expected such a heart-felt reply. Much moved, Lord Hallcroft lifted her gloved fingers to his lips. "So do I, Gwen. So do I."

Chapter Eight

A couple of days later, with the exception of Frances who habitually took her chocolate in bed, the family was enjoying breakfast together. The butler entered the breakfast parlor bearing a sealed note for Lord Hallcroft. His lordship took it, nodding his thanks. He glanced at the penned address. "Why, it's from Aunt Sophronia."

Lady Hallcroft and William looked in surprise across the breakfast table at his lordship. Lady Hallcroft's first thought was that Lady Eagleton had experienced some crisis in health.

It was left to Lady Maria to express Gwen's unvoiced concern. She said with a tiny frown, "I hope that dear Sophronia is not taken ill."

"Not she! The old tartar is pluck to the backbone. She'll outlive us all," said William with conviction.

"William, pray speak more respectfully of your aunt," said Lady Maria with mild reproof.

William merely grinned at his parent and renewed his enthusiastic attack on his steak and kidneys.

Meanwhile, Lord Hallcroft had slit the seal with his knife and opened the sheet. An expression of mild interest on his face, he read it. When he raised his head, he looked directly across at his wife. "Lady Eagleton requests that Gwendolyn visit her this afternoon."

William looked up, his expression one of astonishment. "My word!"

Lady Hallcroft was equally astonished. "I, my lord? Are you quite certain?"

A glint of amusement lighting his eyes, Lord Hallcroft nodded somberly. "Yes, I'm certain. You don't mind, do you, Gwen? It would mean a great deal to me if you could cater to my aunt's wishes."

"Don't do it, Gwen," recommended William. "The old lady probably means to eat you."

"Really, William!" murmured Lady Maria disapprovingly.

"Don't be silly, William," said Lady Hallcroft. She turned back to Lord Hallcroft. "Of course I shall go. If you think I should, my lord."

Even as she acquiesced, however, she reflected on the multitude of things that still needed to be seen to before Lord Hallcroft's guests were due to arrive.

"I would greatly appreciate it, my lady." With a smile, Lord Hallcroft added, "Despite William's disparate feelings on the subject, I do not suspect my aunt of having designs against you."

"It's just that the old lady always put me in mind of the conniving hag out of the village fables," said William cheerfully. "You know, where the wicked old woman lures the unsuspecting children into her hovel and then eats them."

"I knew I shouldn't have allowed that lax tutor for you to remain," said Lady Maria, frowning at her younger son. "Now see what has become of it."

Lord Hallcroft and William laughed. Lady Hallcroft joined in, but even as she was laughing she hoped the visit to Lady Eagleton didn't take up too much of her day. There were so many details yet to be finished for the house party.

She thought that if she set off directly after luncheon, she could probably wind up her visit to Lady Eagleton and return before the evening was too far along, especially since the moon was out, which would make it easier to see driving the carriage.

LADY EAGLETON RECEIVED Gwen in the parlor. "Thank you for coming, Lady Hallcroft. I'm in your debt," said Lady Eagleton in a formal tone.

"Not at all, my lady," murmured Lady Hallcroft. She tried not to feel resentment and impatience over the situation, recognizing that her attitude would not be conducive to an agreeable visit. She was still wondering at the urgency of Lady Eagleton's request. She could not conceive why her ladyship had asked for her to come at all. They had only just met.

She was not left long in suspense.

After Lady Eagleton had inquired after her wishes concerning hot tea and all was ordered to her ladyship's satisfaction, she dismissed the butler. When the door had quietly closed behind the butler, Lady Eagleton turned to her reluctant guest. "You will undoubtedly think me to be naught but a foolish old woman. And selfish, too! But the truth is, it's lonely for me during the holiday. It's not like it was when Lord Eagleton was alive. We had no surviving children, yet we managed to be quite merry during the Christmas season because we surrounded ourselves with friends and neighbors. We always had the house beautifully decorated and we set a table that would bid fair to make one's eyes bulge from its extravagance."

Lady Eagleton was silent a moment as she reflected on past glories. Then she glanced once more at Lady Hallcroft, almost apologetically. "It scarcely seems worth the effort to muster the household to decorate this great empty house and direct the cook to make up a menu when it's only for myself."

"Oh, Lady Eagleton." Lady Hallcroft was dismayed, her ready sympathies instantly stirred. She felt that certainly no one should have to be alone during the Christmas holidays. In light of Lady Eagleton's lonely circumstances, her own pining for her family seemed petty at best. After all, she had Lord Hallcroft and the others at Hallcroft Manor.

"I had hoped that if I could impose on your good nature, you might help me organize for the holiday and then I could take more pleasure in the process," said Lady Eagleton, a bit gruffly. "I wished to have some of the neighbors in and of course I should like my tenants to have a Christmas feast as we used to do in the old days."

Lady Hallcroft's heart completely melted and with it the last of her resentment disappeared. She leaned over to give Lady Eagleton a swift hug and smiled at her. "My dear ma'am! Of course I shall help you! You have only to tell me what you wish to have done."

Lady Eagleton had been startled by Lady Hallcroft's spontaneous show of affection, but she was by no means displeased. She quickly recovered her equilibrium. "Well, then! Let us have in my staff and not waste another moment of this wonderful day." She pulled on the bell. As she smiled at Lady Hallcroft, her faded eyes were sparkling with anticipation.

Having already been through the process once, Gwen confidently set forth several suggestions which instantly found favor with Lady Eagleton. Her ladyship commissioned her upper staff to see that Lady Hallcroft's directions were followed to the letter. Soon messages were sent to the village with orders for meats and cheeses and sundry other items that were needed for the tenants' feast.

As for Lady Eagleton, she set herself the task of writing out in her beautiful copperplate all the invitations for a special evening to which she requested the presence of all the neighborhood. Her invitation to her tenants was carried by word of mouth by her steward, who returned to report that her ladyship's message had generated much excitement.

The servants became worn out with rushing here and there, fetching and carrying, cleaning and polishing, but they caught the excitement. It had been many years since Lady Eagleton's household had seen such a bustle and it quite reminded the older servants of better days before Lord Eagleton had succumbed to a long debilitating illness.

Up went the fir garlands and bows and other symbols of the season, creating a festive air in the dignified house which had all within it's walls exchanging smiles.

Gwen was not unaffected. She loved the Christmas holidays and the cheerful season and all of its attendant celebrations. Between consulting with Lady Eagleton and seeing to all the details for the elderly lady, she scarcely had a moment for reflection.

She thoroughly enjoyed herself.

When the afternoon had drawn on, Lady Eagleton pronounced it time for them to rest from their labors. "I'm exhausted, my dear, but happily so. You have made such a difference and I'm very happy with the result. It has been a long time since I have held a gala evening, but I hope to show my neighbors that I am still to be counted a superb hostess," said Lady Eagleton. "I trust that when my invitation arrives at Hallcroft, you and the rest of the family will attend."

"I'm certain that Lord Hallcroft will be delighted, ma'am. He holds you in too much affection to do otherwise, as do I," said Lady Hallcroft with a smile. "As for myself, I'm quite looking forward to it. I do love the Christmas season and the cheerful faces and lovely carols."

"You'll drag William and Frances along with you, of course," said Lady Eagleton with a show of her teeth. "They have always been a bit frightened of me, you know."

Lady Hallcroft laughed. "I've no doubt of it, and perhaps Lady Maria is, too?"

Lady Eagleton cackled. "Oh, aye! I revel in a certain reputation amongst my relations, but perhaps my Christmas gala will smooth their alarms."

The two ladies took a companionable late tea together, at the conclusion of which Lady Hallcroft felt it was time to take her leave. She informed Lady Eagleton of her decision and her ladyship nodded. "I shall ring for a message to be taken round to the stables for your carriage."

The ladies conversed easily for several minutes while Lady Hallcroft put on her pelisse and gloves. Then the door opened and the butler ushered in Lord Hallcroft's coachman. "My lady, the coachman wishes to speak to Lady Hallcroft."

Lady Hallcroft was surprised. She glanced at Lady Eagleton, who merely raised her brows. "What is it, Wheaton?"

"My lady, one of the leaders has strained a hock. I fear that if we are to set out directly, his lordship's horse will come up permanently lame," said the coachman in a respectful manner.

"Oh, dear! But when shall we be able to leave, then?" asked Lady Hallcroft. She was naturally concerned for the horse but it dismayed her that she would be getting back to the manor later than she had anticipated. All of her forgotten anxieties began to seep back to her.

The coachman cleared his throat and said hoarsely, "I regret, my lady, but it would be best if the horse were to rest overnight."

"Overnight! It is not possible! I must get back before nightfall," exclaimed Lady Hallcroft, her dismay becoming full-blown.

The coachman shook his head.

"Perhaps I could borrow a horse from you, dear Lady Eagleton, and leave the lame one here to recover?"

Lady Eagleton and the coachman exchanged a swift glance it was impossible for her to interpret.

"I'm sorry, my dear. It's not possible. My team are ill-tempered beasts and will only work in tandem with their own," said Lady Eagleton with finality.

"That be true, my lady," said the coachman quickly. "Her ladyship's horses are likely to kick out and maim his lordship's team."

"Could you not send me home in your own carriage, then?" suggested Lady Hallcroft impatiently. It seemed a simple enough solution.

Lady Eagleton shook her head. "I fear not. Tomorrow is always the date I reserve to discharge my responsibility toward my tenants at this time of year. I have several visits to make beginning at first light. I understand that one or two of my tenants are ill. Forgive me, Gwendolyn, but I really cannot put off such errands as those."

"No, of course not," said Lady Hallcroft automatically. She looked at Lady Eagleton rather helplessly. "But then, what do you suggest, ma'am?"

"I don't consider the matter to be a problem, my dear. You must stay the night, of course," said Lady Eagleton coolly. "We shall allow the poor horse to rest overnight and in the morning it will probably be much recovered. Isn't that what you implied, coachman?"

The coachman nodded and turned his concerned gaze on Lady Hallcroft. In the face of the man's obvious distress over the circumstances, Gwen unhappily shrugged her shoulders. "I suppose there is nothing else to be done."

The coachman appeared immensely relieved and bowed himself out of the room.

"I understand that you're upset, Gwendolyn," said Lady Eagleton. "However, it is only a few hours, after all. My nephew will do very well without you for that long!"

"It's not that!" exclaimed Lady Hallcroft, turning impetuously toward the old lady. "My lord commissioned me to plan a house party for all of his influential friends. There's still so much to do! What if I should fail?" She unconsciously twisted her hands together.

Silence reigned for several seconds as Lady Eagleton regarded her guest with a blank expression. Under that unblinking regard, Lady Hallcroft flushed. In a suffocated voice, she said, "Forgive me, my lady. I shouldn't have burst out in such a fashion."

Lady Eagleton nodded and held out her hand. "Come, my dear. I shall put you into the capable hands of my housekeeper. She shall take you up to your room, where you can rest before dinner."

Lady Hallcroft acquiesced to Lady Eagleton's suggestion, but she was too keyed up to nap. After the maid had left her, she simply sat in front of the fire on a footstool, thinking. She turned over and over in her mind what had happened, and she kept coming back to the swift glance exchanged by Lady Eagleton and the coachman. It was almost as though they were co-conspirators, their goal to keep her at Lady Eagleton's residence. "But what nonsense!"

Lady Hallcroft felt stupid for even entertaining such a thought. However, the nagging suspicion was not quite stilled.

At dinner, Lady Eagleton exerted herself to be an amusing hostess. She began recounting several more of her youthful adventures, creating such fascination for Lady Hallcraft that she actually forgot her problem.

It was not until she had retired to bed, attired in a gown borrowed from her hostess, when she again began to fret over her inability to return to Hallcroft Manor. She didn't think that she would be able to sleep. However, it had been a long day filled with activities and even her natural anxiety over being unable to return home could not keep her awake.

The morning dawned cold and with a lowering sky. Lady Eagleton invited Gwen to accompany her on her visits to the estate tenants.

Lady Hallcroft agreed, more out of civility than desire. However, by the time that she and Lady Eagleton had made the rounds and handed out the practical gifts which Lady Eagleton had prepared for each family, Lady Hallcroft was in a much better frame of mind. She understood by then that Lady Eagleton's feeling of obligation toward her tenants was deeply ingrained and that because of it her ladyship was well-liked. In fact, at each small thatch-roofed dwelling it was obvious that the tenants and their families had all awaited her ladyship's arrival. Without exception they had come out-of-doors as soon as Lady Eagleton's carriage stopped.

Lady Hallcroft realized that the tenants knew, from long-standing tradition, what date that Lady Eagleton would come, bearing small gifts for them and their children and to talk with them. It would have been a bitter disappointment to all if Lady Eagleton had not appeared.

Lady Hallcroft was ashamed she had harbored unkind thoughts over Lady Eagleton's refusal to put off her own responsibilities in order to lend out her carriage. She quite understood now the reasoning behind her ladyship's refusal. Lady Eagleton was all too aware what her absence on that particular date would mean.

But perhaps, thought Lady Hallcroft hopefully, since those obligations were now fulfilled, Lady Eagleton would be more amenable. Surely there could not now be any objection to the lending of the carriage for her use. Lady Hallcroft resolved to put the question to her hostess after they had warmed themselves over tea.

However, the weather took a capricious hand in Lady Hallcroft's plans. Even before the ladies had returned to the manor house, the wind began blowing hard. It was bitingly cold and flurries of snow stung their faces even as the ladies hurried inside.

By the time Lady Eagleton and Gwen had put off their damp wraps and begun to warm themselves by the fire, waiting for tea to be served, the snowstorm was in full gale.

Chapter Nine

"I suspect this weather will keep you tied here yet a while, Gwendolyn," remarked Lady Eagleton, sipping at her cup.

Lady Hallcroft hated to admit it, but she feared Lady Eagleton was correct. When she looked out the window, it was only to see a curtain of impenetrable white. There was no way her coachman would be able to see the road on such a day.

"I'm sorry, my dear," said Lady Eagleton gently.

Lady Hallcroft summoned up a smile. "It's unfortunate, indeed. However, I trust that you and I shall pass the time well enough, ma'am."

"That's the spirit, girl," said Lady Eagleton with a slight smile.

The storm howled all night and then tapered off into a steady fall of snow. The day following was marked by weak sunshine and Lady Hallcroft's rising hope that the snow had at last run its course. She sent word down to the stables and was vastly relieved to learn that the lame horse was indeed recovered. At luncheon, when Lady Eaglton came down from her rooms, Lady Hallcroft announced that she would be leaving within the hour.

Lady Eagleton's sharp eyes shot to her guest's face but her expression remained perfectly civil. "Of course, my dear. When my dresser brought me word this morning that the weather had begun to clear, I knew at once that you would be off. I've enjoyed our time together. I hope that you, too, have been amused?"

"Of course, ma'am. It has been a pleasant visit indeed." Lady Hallcroft was sincere. Despite her restive desire to return to Hallcroft Manor, she had found much to busy herself with and to entertain her while she was marooned in Lady Eagleton's company. "I wish that you would come stay with us at Hallcroft sometime during the holiday, my lady."

Lady Eagleton looked surprised. Then her expression softened. A bit gruffly, she said, "Thank you, my dear. You've no notion what your invitation means to me, especially after such a trying time as you've had."

She paused. "I expect that some of your guests will have arrived already by the time you make your return."

Lady Hallcroft nodded, her unhappiness rushing back on her. "I fear so, my lady. I had so wanted to make certain of all of the details before the house party began."

"Never mind. Lady Maria isn't completely useless. I've no doubt that she arranged all just as you had given orders for it to be done," said Lady Eagleton. "You've wrought a minor miracle here. Therefore I would be astonished indeed if your staff disregarded any of your superb direction."

Lady Hallcroft was heartened by Lady Eagleton's encouragement and she was able to take leave of the inimitable old lady with good spirits. However, as the carriage set off and carried her ever nearer to the manor, her insecurities came creeping back. What if something had gone wrong? What if Lord Hallcroft was displeased with how the house party had been launched? And how could his lordship send her off at such a time, when he must have known how anxiously she had been planning the arrangements for his guests?

Snowflakes flashed past the glass, winking in the late-afternoon sunlight like so many bits of shiny tinsel. The white fields and hedgerows were marked by tall pristine drifts. It was an enchanting prospect, but Gwen was not in the least appreciative.

When the carriage drew up at the front steps of the manor, Lady Hallcroft waited impatiently for the door to be opened and the iron step to be let down. She scarcely waited for the footman to help her down to the icy gravel before she swept up the front steps.

She stopped when the door opened and Lord Hallcroft stepped outside, closing the front door behind him.

Gwen eyed him somewhat resentfully. Lord Haffcroft didn't seem the least put out that she had been gone nearly three days. She was still hurt that he had sent her away so easily on the visit to his aunt, especially on the eve of her debut as hostess. Nor did he express a shred of emotion at seeing her back. He simply stared at her.

A horrible suspicion raised its ugly head. Surely Lord Hallcroft had not fallen out of love with her. Surely he still felt some particle of affection for her! She thought it was despicable to have such creeping doubts at the holiday season, which had always been the most joyous time of the year for her.

"I hope you enjoyed your little visit," said Lord Hallcroft, breaking his silence at last. "It was a bit longer than I had anticipated it would be."

Gwen nearly stamped her foot. With an effort she managed to speak civilly. "In truth it was becoming rather tedious, my lord." She was glad to hear how cool her voice was, but at the same time she was saddened. Was she doomed for the remainder of her life to such cold exchanges?

Lord Hallcroft pulled a wide silk scarf out of his coat pocket. "I have a surprise for you, my lady, but I don't wish you to see it until I'm ready to reveal it. Pray indulge me for a moment and allow me to blindfold you."

"You want to what?" asked Lady Hallcroft, stiffening with outrage, as her thoughts veered between disbelief and hurt. She could scarcely credit it that he wanted to play at a silly parlor game. She was standing in the cold with snowflakes melting in her hair!

"Please, Gwendolyn," said Lord Hallcroft softly.

She found she couldn't resist the appeal in his voice, nor the light in his eyes. "Oh, very well!" she snapped, and hated that she sounded petulant.

Lord Hallcroft didn't appear to notice, but turned her around to tie the scarf securely over her eyes. "Can you see anything?"

"No, of course not," said Lady Hallcroft shortly.

"Then I shall lead you indoors now."

"Good! I'm chilled by standing about," she said. One part of her was appalled by her sharpness but she didn't care. She was very, very hurt that Lord Hallcroft didn't seem the least bit bothered by their separation. On the contrary, he *wanted to play a silly game.* Gwen rebelliously thought that she was not in the mood for games.

Lady Hallcroft heard the front door open and felt Lord Hallcroft's hand under her elbow, guiding her. She stepped inside cautiously, her hands half raised in front of her.

Lord Hallcroft drew her slowly forward and Lady Hallcroft heard the front door close behind her again. She thought that the footman must have shut it. Then Lord Hallcroft carefully turned her in a new direction and she realized he was leading her into the drawing room. She heard a soft giggle, swiftly silenced, and she felt humiliated that she was being made such a spectacle of in front of the household.

On the other hand, she was also becoming rather curious. Lord Hallcroft had said that he had a surprise for her. She could not imagine what it could be, but her heart began to beat more rapidly.

"This is far enough."

Lady Hallcroft felt his strong fingers working at the knot at the back of her head. She waited with bated breath until she could see again.

The silk scarf dropped from her eyes. Gwen gasped. Tears smarted in her eyes. She was standing in front of a semicircle of her family, which crowded the drawing room from wall to wall. Lady Maria, William and Frances were there, too. In unison the entire company shouted, "Merry Christmas! Merry Christmas!"

"Mama! Papa!" Gwen shrieked, and rushed forward. She was engulfed in the arms of her family as they all began speaking animatedly together. She couldn't stop exclaiming at their unexpected presence.

Lord Hallcroft stood a little to one side, enjoying the sight. He was included by one and then another, all of whom congratulated him on a successful surprise.

Taking advantage of a thinning in the circle surrounding Lady Hallcroft, Lady Maria went forward to draw her daughter-in-law into a gentle embrace. "Merry Christmas, dear, dear Gwendolyn."

"Thank you, ma'am," said Lady Hallcroft happily. Meeting her mother-in-law's smiling gaze, she realized that Lady Maria did indeed regard her with affection. Her already full heart overflowed. Lady Maria stepped back, and Gwen was once again engulfed by her family.

It eventually dawned on Lady Hallcroft, as she listened to her brother and sisters and their spouses, that they were expecting to make an extended stay. Gwen finally voiced the question that had loomed larger and larger in her mind. She turned to Lord Hallcroft in confusion. "But I don't understand, my lord! I thought we were to have quite a different party of guests."

"It's my Christmas gift to you, Gwendolyn."

Lady Hallcroft looked around again at all of her loved ones, the shimmering of tears in her eyes blurring their dear faces. She could scarcely believe it was true, that she was to celebrate the holiday with them all. And she owed it all to one person.

Impulsively she turned and flung her arms around her husband's neck. "I love you so!" she declared.

There arose indulgent, good-natured laughter all around. "Merry Christmas, Gwen!" shouted William.

Lord Hallcroft was seen to turn red, but he grinned also. "Then you don't mind my subterfuge in sending you away from the house?"

"Oh, I did! And later I shall scold you monstrously for making me so very unhappy and confused," said Lady Hallcroft. She suddenly realized what he had said and her mouth rounded with astonishment. "Do you mean that Lady Eagleton knew – that was why she sent for me?"

Lord Hallcroft looked a little uncomfortable. He regarded his wife's expression anxiously, unsure how she might react. "It was all an elaborate plot from the very beginning. I enlisted the help of my family and Lady Eagleton and your parents. My mother scolded me for employing such a stratagem. I confess, it was rather Machiavellian. Can you forgive me for causing you unhappiness?"

"Oh, I do! But I think – yes, I think I shall punish you just a little, my lord," said Lady Hallcroft.

She saw that Lord Hallcroft was looking both wary and uncertain. Her eyes gleamed with laughter. She gave a slow smile. "You're standing under the mistletoe bough, my lord." Thereupon she kissed him full on the lips, amid much laughter and hand-clapping. Fleetingly, she wondered what he would make of her patently public display of affection, but he surprised her.

Lord Hallcroft caught her up in his arms and proved he was very much a man of the moment. Looking deep into her astonished eyes, he proclaimed roundly, "You are the one and only love of my heart, Gwen."

Then he kissed her in a way that she would remember all of her life.

Other Books by Gayle Buck
The Righteous Rakehell
Mutual Consent
Willowswood Match
The Demon Rake
Love's Masquerade
The Fleeing Heiress Cassandra's Deception
Belle's Beau
Magnificent Match
Honor Besieged
Lady Althea's Bargain
Love for Lucinda
Frederica's Folly
Chester Charade
Cupid's Choice
Lord Darlington's Darling
A Chance Encounter
The Waltzing Widow
Tempting Sarah
Lord John's Lady
Lord Rathbone's Flirt
The Desperate Viscount
Hearts Betrayed
The Hidden Heart
Miss Dower's Paragon
Lady Cecily's Scheme
<u>Regency Tales</u>
Old Acquaintances Holybrooke Curse
Christmas Cheer Season of Joy
Regency Tales: Christmas Collection
Alegria Navidena
<u>Regency Duets</u>

Cassandra's Deception & Belle's Beau
The Hidden Heart & The Desperate Viscount
Chester Charade & The Fleeing Heiress
The Waltzing Widow & Hearts Betrayed
Lord John's Lady & The Magnificent Match
The Holybrooke Curse & Cupid's Choice
Regency Tales: Christmas Collection

Don't miss out!

Visit the website below and you can sign up to receive emails whenever Gayle Buck publishes a new book. There's no charge and no obligation.

https://books2read.com/r/B-A-AISJ-SMHDB

BOOKS2READ

Connecting independent readers to independent writers.

Also by Gayle Buck

Tempting Sarah
The Waltzing Widow
The Holybrooke Curse
Season of Joy
Hearts Betrayed
Chistmas Cheer
Old Acquaintances
Mutual Consent
The Chester Charade
The Desperate Viscount
Lady Althea's Bargain
Fredericka's Folly
Love for Lucinda
Lord Darlington's Darling
The Demon Rake
Lord Rathbone's Flirt
Miss Dower's Paragon
Belle's Beau
Cassandra's Deception
Love's Masquerade
The Righteous Rakehell
A Magnificent Match
The Hidden Heart
Willowswood Match
A Chance Encounter

The Fleeing Heiress
Lady Cecily's Scheme
Cupid's Choice
Lord John's Lady
Honor Besieged